For the great Dads—SM & EK

For my dad, Ian, with love—MO

Me and My Dad

By **Sally Morgan** and **Ezekiel Kwaymullina**
Illustrated by **Matt Ottley**

LITTLE HARE
www.littleharebooks.com

My dad is not afraid of sharp shells,

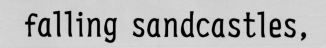

falling sandcastles,

crazy crabs,

angry dogs ...

or giant waves.

My dad is not afraid of slimy seaweed,

stinging jellyfish,

slithering sea snakes ...

or hungry sharks.

But my dad is afraid of one thing.

I'm not.

Dad says we are heroes together.

Little Hare Books
an imprint of
Hardie Grant Egmont
85 High Street
Prahran, Victoria 3181, Australia

www.littleharebooks.com

National Library of Australia
Cataloguing-in-Publication entry

Morgan, Sally, 1951-
Me and my dad / Sally Morgan, Ezekiel Kwaymullina; illustrator, Matt Ottley.
9781921541810 (hbk.)
For primary school age.
Fathers - Juvenile fiction.
Fathers and sons - Juvenile fiction.
Kwaymullina, Ezekiel.
Ottley, Matthew.
A823.3

Designed by Vida & Luke Kelly
Produced by Pica Digital, Singapore
Printed through Phoenix Offset
Printed in Shen Zhen, Guangdong Province, China, May 2010

5 4 3 2 1